Lucy was Henrietta's best friend.

"My tooth, Henrietta. My wobbly tooth came out last night. I put it under the pillow and the tooth fairy left me twenty pence."

"Great," replied Henrietta, without any real enthusiasm.

"How's your wobbly tooth then?" asked Lucy. For a second Henrietta did not reply. Then she jumped up and began to hop around the hallway.

"Of course! You're a genius, Lucy. My wobbly tooth. Why didn't I think of it before? Sorry, I've got to go. I've had an idea."

Henrietta can't wait for her wobbly tooth to fall out, and for the tooth fairy to call. Then she thinks up a plan to make sure the tooth falls out quickly:..

Henrietta and the Tooth Fairy is the first in a series of books about the mischievous Henrietta and her family.

Look out for the second title about Henrietta,
coming soon from Young Corgi Books:

HENRIETTA'S BUBBLE TROUBLE

HENRIETTA AND THE TOOTH FAIRY
is one of a series of books specially selected to
be suitable for beginner readers, BY MYSELF
BOOKS.

HENRIETTA AND
THE TOOTH FAIRY

HENRIETTA AND THE TOOTH FAIRY

Stan Cullimore

Illustrated by John Farman

YOUNG CORGI BOOKS

HENRIETTA AND THE TOOTH FAIRY

A YOUNG CORGI BOOK 0 552 52745 9

First published in Great Britain by Piccadilly Press Ltd.

PRINTING HISTORY
Piccadilly Press edition published 1991
Young Corgi edition published 1993

Young Corgi Books are published by Transworld Publishers Ltd.,
61–63 Uxbridge Road, Ealing, London W5 5SA, in Australia by
Transworld Publishers (Australia) Pty. Ltd., 15–23 Helles Avenue,
Moorebank, NSW 2170, and in New Zealand by Transworld Publishers
(N.Z.) Ltd., 3 William Pickering Drive, Albany, Auckland.

Printed and bound in Great Britain by
Cox & Wyman Ltd., Reading, Berks.

CONTENTS

STORY ONE

LEARNING TO SWIM

"Henrietta. Wakey, wakey, or we will be late." Henrietta's mother put down the tray of green bananas she was carrying and opened the curtains in Henrietta's room. Henrietta opened one eye.

"Late for what?"

"You haven't forgotten what day it is, have you?" said her mother. "Today is Saturday." Henrietta pulled a face.

"Ratburgers," she groaned as she sat up in bed. "I hate Saturdays."

Up until the last two weeks, Henrietta had loved Saturdays. But now she had changed her mind. Saturday was the day when all the family went to the swimming pool and Henrietta had her swimming lesson.

"Boring," grumped Henrietta as she ate her green bananas in bed. "I hate

water and I don't want to learn to swim."
As her mother turned to leave the room
Henrietta put her banana skin under the
pillow and folded her arms.

Her mother sighed.

"Daniel can swim."

Henrietta snorted. "He's a show-off."
Her mother sighed once more.

"Daniel isn't a show-off. He is just a
good swimmer. You could be a good
swimmer, young lady, if you just tried a
little bit harder at your swimming lessons.
And stopped acting like such a baby."

She went off to make breakfast for
Baby-Rose and Dad.

*   *   *

Henrietta lay in bed and looked at the
ceiling.

"It's not fair."

Suddenly she jumped up and began to

dance around the room. "What a brilliant idea," she cried. "No more swimming lessons for me. I've got a secret plan. Yippee!"

She picked up her felt-tip pens and her box of blue balloons. Then she skipped into the kitchen.

After breakfast the whole family set off for the swimming pool. Henrietta, her mother and her father pushing Baby-Rose in the buggy. Her sensible brother Daniel was carrying the towels.

"How come Henrietta never carries anything?" asked Daniel. "I'm always the helpful one."

"What a creep," muttered Henrietta. She was never helpful.

Usually, when they walked to the swimming pool, Henrietta stayed at the back . . . holding a tickling stick. And sometimes, only sometimes, it would ever

so accidentally tickle Daniel's legs as he
walked.

"Stop it, Henrietta," Daniel would say.
"Stop it or I'll tell."

"Oh sorry, Daniel," Henrietta would
reply. Then the tickling stick would
accidentally tickle Daniel again.

But today Henrietta ran along in front holding onto her felt-tip pens.

"Now where did I put my balloons? Ah, here they are." She had hidden them in one of her pockets.

*　　　*　　　*

When she got to the swimming pool Henrietta looked around her. The others hadn't finished changing yet.

"Better make sure that no-one can see me," she thought. Quickly she blew up a balloon and using her felt-tip pen she drew on it a pair of eyes, just like her own eyes. Then a nose, just like her own nose.

Then she placed the balloon in the swimming pool and pushed it, so that it floated right out into the middle of the deep end. She sniggered to herself and hid behind a chair.

Soon the rest of the family arrived.

"Look," cried Mum, pointing at the balloon. "What on earth is that?"

Henrietta's father gasped and started to laugh. Then he nudged Daniel and winked at Mum.

"Good grief," he said, "I think it's Henrietta. Doesn't she look strange. Her face has gone blue!" Behind the chair Henrietta sniggered and snorted.

"My plan is working. No more stupid swimming lessons for me." Her father picked up Baby-Rose and pointed at the balloon.

"Look at your big sister. Isn't she clever learning to swim all by herself." Behind the chair Henrietta was having to hold her nose to stop herself from laughing.

"Yes I am clever," she chuckled, "and so is my plan." She scratched her nose.

Her mother waved at the balloon.

"Henrietta," she laughed, "you are a clever little girl. I told you that you could be a good swimmer if you tried." But Henrietta did not hear them all laughing at the balloon, she was too busy laughing herself.

"They think I'm in the water," she snorted, "but I'm not."

* * *

By now she was laughing so hard that she could not stand up.

"Hehehe," she laughed. "Hohoho." She noticed her nose was feeling all tickly. "That's funny," she laughed. "It feels as if someone is tickling my nose with a tickling stick, ah . . . tickling stick, ah . . . Oh no, not my sneezy nose." She tried to hold it with both hands. But it was too late.

"Atishoo." She did a Henrietta hyper-sneeze that blew her over the chair and into the swimming pool. Right on top of the balloon.

*　　*　　*

When she opened her eyes Henrietta saw her mother and father and even Baby-Rose all staring at her.

"Hahaha. Fooled you," cried Henrietta. "You thought that silly balloon was me. Well it wasn't. I was hiding behind the chair all the time."

Then she saw her sensible brother Daniel.

He was standing behind the chair, holding the biggest, tickliest tickling

stick Henrietta had ever seen.

"You knew all along," cried Henrietta.
"It was you tickling my nose, wasn't it.
You made me sneeze and fall into the
water. And I can't even swim. HELP."
Just then Henrietta noticed something.

"I'm swimming. Mum, Dad, look.

I can swim." Her mother smiled.

"I told you that if you tried you could swim, Henrietta." But Henrietta did not hear her. She was too busy sticking out her tongue at Daniel.

STORY TWO

THE NEW BLUE SHOES

"Henrietta, just look at your shoes," said Henrietta's mother . . . "They're filthy. Why can't you be more like your brother Daniel and look after your things."

Daniel looked up from the latest issue of *Computer World* and smiled his most charming smile.

"Creep," thought Henrietta. She looked down at her shoes. There was nothing wrong with them at all. "I like

wearing dirty shoes. I've just found a
puddle with the stickiest, slimiest green
mud in the whole world."

Her sensible brother Daniel laughed
his most annoying laugh.

"I never get my shoes dirty, do I,
Mummy?"

Henrietta stuck out her tongue and

pulled a face.

"I don't want to be sensible like Daniel. I like being the way I am. It suits me. I'm a dirty person."

Henrietta's mother snorted. "I don't care what you say, young lady. This afternoon you and I are going to town to buy you some new shoes. Now clean up those filthy things."

Daniel crossed his eyes and thumbed

his nose when Mum wasn't looking.

"Some people never get into trouble for having dirty shoes," Henrietta sighed. Suddenly she grinned one of her cheekiest grins.

She had just thought of a plan to wipe the smile off Daniel's face.

* * *

After dinner Henrietta and her mother

walked Daniel to the park. He was going
to play football with some of his friends.
When they got there Henrietta helped
Daniel to put his shoes into his bag.

"I'll hang it up for you if you like," she
said. Before Daniel could answer, she
had run off with the bag and disappeared
into the pavilion.

When she emerged she looked very
cheeky indeed.

*   *   *

Henrietta liked going to town,
especially when they went by bus. It was
fun. You could put your feet under the
seat in front and pretend you were the
driver.

"Henrietta," cried her mother, "get
your feet out from there. Your shoes are
almost as dirty as they were this morning.
Why can't you be more like your brother

for once, and think."

"Sorry, Mum," said Henrietta. She lifted up her feet and muttered something under her breath. "We'll soon see about that Daniel, won't we?" But she said it so quietly that her mother did not hear.

When they got to the shoe shop, Henrietta looked at the rows and rows of shoes in the window and pulled a face.

"Ratburgers," she cried. "They're all so boring. I hate them!" Her mother was beginning to get cross.

"Boring. I'll give you boring, Henrietta, if you don't start behaving yourself." She started walking towards some really ugly black shoes.

The manager, a tall thin man with flies buzzing around his ears, then started to show them every single black shoe he had. Henrietta hated them all.

At last the man stood up and wiped his ears with his handkerchief.

"I'm very sorry, Madam," he said to Henrietta's mother. "But we have no more black shoes in the shop." He glared at Henrietta.

She didn't hear him. She was too busy staring at the fly that had just landed on her nose.

"Oh no! Not my sneezy nose," cried Henrietta. She tried to flick the fly away. But it was too late.

"Atishoo." She did a Henrietta hyper-sneeze that blew all the shoes off the wall and into a huge great heap on the floor. And there right on top of the pile, were the best, most brilliant shoes in the whole world.

* * *

"Wow," cried Henrietta, "they're fantastic." They were bright blue with orange spots and pink laces. "Can I have those ones, Mum? *Please!*"

"They'll be dirty in half an hour. Black is the best colour for you, Henrietta."

"Please Mum, *please.*" Henrietta put on her most charming smile and flashed her eyelashes, "I'll keep them really clean. I will, promise I will."

* * *

As Henrietta and her mother walked back to the bus stop Henrietta went on tiptoes all the way.

"I'm never going to get these new blue shoes dirty," she said. "I'm going to look after them." And she really meant it. All the way home on the bus she kept her feet well away from the seat in front.

She even wiped her shoes with a tissue after they accidentally touched against her mother's shopping basket.

When they got to the front door Henrietta burst in to show her father the bright blue shoes with orange spots and pink laces.

"I'm going to look after them," she said. "Honest I am, Dad." Her father smiled.

"That will make a nice change."

"Henrietta might even be getting as sensible as her brother Daniel," said her mother. Just then the door opened and in walked Daniel. He looked most unhappy.

"Daniel," said his father, "your shoes. They're filthy!" They were too. They were covered from tip to toe in sticky, slimy green mud.

"Those shoes are a disgrace," cried his mother. "I can't believe it. They're far worse than anything Henrietta has come home with." Henrietta smiled one of her happiest, cheekiest smiles.

"I'm just going to play in the garden," she said. "Don't worry, I'll keep these new blue shoes really clean."

*   *   *

They never did find out how Daniel's shoes got so mucky. But I'll tell you what I think. I think a cheeky little someone must have covered them in green mud while they were in Daniel's bag. Now, whoever would do a thing like that, I wonder . . .

STORY THREE

HOW TO BECOME A NICER PERSON

"What on earth do you think you're doing, Henrietta?" shouted Dad.

Henrietta stopped and smiled at her father.

"I'm skipping. Watch." She began to skip once more. Her father's face went bright red, like it always did when he got cross.

"I know you're skipping, Henrietta," he sighed. "But why are you using two of Daniel's ties as a skipping rope?"

"Because one tie isn't long enough on its own. So I had to put two together." Henrietta carried on jumping.

Her father gasped. Henrietta noticed his teeth were now clenched and he spoke very slowly.

"What! You know better than to use Daniel's ties as a skipping rope. And I've told you before not to take anything from Daniel's room without asking first. Get to your room this instant. And don't come out until you've learnt how to behave properly." He grabbed the ties. Henrietta stomped upstairs.

* * *

When she got to her room Henrietta slammed the door and yanked open the cupboard.

"This is going to be really boring," she groaned. "Now what do I do?" She began

to rummage through her toys. "Hello.
What's this?" A book had fallen down the
back of the shelf and been forgotten.
Henrietta picked it up. It was called
How to Become a Nicer Person. Henrietta
opened it and in spite of herself, began to

read. According to the man who wrote it, the easiest way to become a nicer person was to do three good deeds every day.

"I could do that," thought Henrietta. "Easy." She looked at herself in the mirror and smiled her nicest smile. "If I was to become a nicer person then I would know how to behave properly."

She decided that Dad would have cooled down by now. So she put down the book and went into the kitchen to begin her three good deeds.

*　　*　　*

"Good afternoon, Daniel dearest," she said to her sensible brother, who was carefully feeding Baby-Rose banana and baked beans. Daniel did not reply. He was far too busy. He didn't even look up when Henrietta spoke. Henrietta was just about to stick out her tongue and pull a horrible face to make Baby-Rose cry, when she remembered her book and the three good deeds. She smiled.

"Do let me help you, Daniel." Before Daniel knew what was happening Henrietta had snatched the spoon and was feeding Baby-Rose all by herself.

"Thank you, Henrietta," said Daniel,

surprised and pleased. "My *Computer World* has just arrived and there's something new I've got to figure out."

Henrietta waved her hand. "Off you go then. You enjoy yourself while I stay here and do all the work."

"You sound just like Mum," muttered Daniel as he opened his *Computer World* and began to read.

* * *

The trouble was that Henrietta was not

as careful as her brother.

"Ratburgers," she muttered as the baked beans slithered from the spoon onto the floor.

"Watch it," yelled Daniel as a bit of banana plopped neatly on to the centre of his *Computer World*.

Baby-Rose laughed. Henrietta lifted her out of the high-chair and left the disaster area.

"For my next good deed," thought Henrietta, "I shall make Mum a nice hot cup of tea in her favourite mug. She loves tea." The trouble was that Henrietta could not find any teabags. She found the Bovril jar though. So she used Bovril instead.

Her mother was in the garden mowing the lawn.

"Thank you, Henrietta. A nice hot cup of tea. My favourite." Henrietta beamed.

"I know it is, Mum. I made it just the way you like." She skipped back into the house. Her mother took a sip of the tea and squawked.

"Yuk. This tea tastes of Bovril. I hate Bovril."

*　　*　　*

In the kitchen Henrietta was dancing around the table.

"Yippee," she cried, "now I have done two good deeds. Only one more and then I will be a nicer person. And even Dad won't be cross with me any more." She wondered what to do next. Suddenly she had an idea.

"I'll tidy my room," she cried. "Dad always says it's so messy it's like a pigsty." Henrietta went into her room and closed the door.

Soon everything was neat and tidy.

There weren't any banana skins under the pillow. Henrietta had put them all in the binbag. She had even swept her collection of crisp packets from under the bed. And her dirty clothes were in the laundry basket.

"There," said Henrietta as some dust floated past her nose. "Finished. Now I have done three good deeds. I've fed Baby-Rose her dinner. I've made Mum a cup of tea and I've tidied my room. That means I've become a nicer ah . . . nicer ah . . . Oh no. Not my sneezy nose." She tried to stop it. But it was too late.

"Atishoo." She did a Henrietta hyper-sneeze that blew the binbag right out of the window. "Oh good! Now I won't have to carry all that rubbish out to the dustbin."

The door opened.

"Hello," said Dad. He looked around

the room and his face brightened. "I must have walked into the wrong room, this can't possibly be yours, Henrietta. It's too tidy."

"Dad," cried Henrietta. "I've done it."

"Done what?" asked Dad.

"My three good deeds. I found a book that said if you want to become a nicer person you have to do three good deeds

every day. And I have. So I've become a nicer person. So now I'll know how to behave properly, won't I?"

*　　*　　*

Just then Daniel appeared.

"I can't read my *Computer World*," he wailed. "The pages are stuck together with banana."

Then Henrietta and her father went into the kitchen, where Henrietta's mother was pouring the contents of her cup down the sink.

"Worst cup of tea I've ever had." She pulled a face. "And you should see what's in the garden. It looks as if someone has emptied a binbag full of crisp packets all over my lovely lawn." Everyone rushed to the window.

"Oh," said Henrietta, "that's where all my rubbish went."

"By the way, what were your three good deeds, Henrietta?" asked Dad. Henrietta looked at the messy lawn. She looked at Daniel's *Computer World* stuck together with banana and she looked at the mug still in her mother's hand.

"My three good deeds," she said. "Hmm, well . . . they weren't really that good. In fact, I've decided not to do any more good deeds. I don't want to become a nicer person. It's too much like hard work. And it never comes out the way you want it to."

Dad laughed, "But what about your book?"

Henrietta shrugged her shoulders. "I'll give it to Daniel, he needs it more than I do."

With that she kissed her father. Then she rushed up the stairs. She had just thought of a brilliant game to play with Daniel's ties!

But this time she would ask him first.

STORY FOUR

THE WOBBLY TOOTH

"I'm never going to have enough money. I might as well give up." Henrietta threw down her piggy bank and sat on her bed. "It's ridiculous. I only need another twenty pence. But Dad's too mean to give it to me."

She was saving up to buy some stripey green laces for her blue shoes and Dad had refused to give her any money unless she kept her room tidy for a whole week.

"I like my room to be messy,"

40

grumbled Henrietta. The door opened and Dad walked in.

"Lucy is on the phone for you." He looked around the room. "Still as messy as ever, I see. You'll never get your twenty pence at this rate. Not that I mind, it saves me money. You know what a mean old Dad I am!" He walked out of the room with his hands in his pockets, as Henrietta ran downstairs to the phone.

* * *

Lucy was Henrietta's best friend.

"My tooth, Henrietta. My wobbly tooth came out last night. I put it under the pillow and the tooth fairy left me twenty pence. Isn't that brilliant? Now I can buy those laces." Lucy was saving up to buy some laces as well.

"Great," replied Henrietta, without any real enthusiasm.

41

"How's your wobbly tooth then?"
asked Lucy. For a second Henrietta did
not reply. Then she jumped up and began
to hop around the hallway.

"Of course! You're a genius, Lucy. My
wobbly tooth. Why didn't I think of it

before. Sorry, I've got to go. I've had an idea." She put down the phone and clapped her hands.

"Now, how do I get this wobbly tooth to come out? Because if I can get it to come out, the tooth fairy will leave me twenty pence and then I will be able to buy my laces. Hmm." She thought for a minute.

"Toffee. Sticky toffee. Dad always says he's surprised my teeth don't fall out when I eat sticky toffee. But where do I get it from?" She frowned. Then she smiled.

She ran upstairs to her room and opened her sock drawer. She began to search through it. "I'm sure I hid some in here last week. Ah! Here it is. Great." She unwrapped the toffee and popped it into her mouth. Then she went downstairs.

*   *   *

"What on earth are you eating?" asked her mother.

"Bicky boffee," replied Henrietta as best she could. It wasn't easy talking with a mouthful of sticky toffee.

"What did you say?"

Henrietta took the toffee out of her mouth and explained.

"Well you can just put it in the bin right now. Why are you eating toffee anyway? It's nearly time for tea."

Henrietta quickly put the toffee in her hanky and pretended to throw it in the bin.

"I know why she's eating sticky toffee," said Daniel. "She wants her wobbly tooth to come out. So she can get twenty pence off the tooth fairy and buy those stupid laces. I heard her talking to Lucy about it."

Henrietta's father snorted.

"The tooth fairy wouldn't be able to get into that room. Let alone find a tooth. It's as messy as a pigsty in there."

Daniel laughed.

"Creep," muttered Henrietta.

After tea Henrietta went up to her room and got the sticky toffee out of her hanky. It was covered in fluff. But Henrietta didn't mind. She popped it into her mouth and began to chew.

*   *   *

A few minutes later she swallowed what was left of the toffee and looked in

the mirror.

"Ratburgers," she cried. Her wobbly tooth was still in place. Just then Daniel walked in carrying a long piece of string.

"I can get rid of that tooth for you, if you like."

Henrietta jumped up. "How?"

"Easy," replied Daniel. "We tie one end of this string around your tooth. I hold the other end and you run towards the bed. When the string goes tight it will pull your tooth out. I've seen it done on television lots of times."

"OK. Let's do it."

Daniel tied the string around Henrietta's wobbly tooth and held onto the other end as tightly as he could.

"Ready?" Henrietta nodded.

"Steady?" Daniel closed his eyes.

"Go!" Henrietta ran towards the bed as fast as she could. The string went tight. Then tighter. Then, it snapped.

There was a shout. "Help." Then a CRASH as Daniel fell backwards and landed head first in the binbag.

"Help," he cried, waving his legs in the air. "Help, I'm stuck." Henrietta sniggered.

"You do look funny, Daniel. Hehehe." She stopped as some dust floated past her nose. "Ah . . . ah . . . Oh no. Not my sneezy nose." She looked for her hanky.

But it was too late.

"Atishoo." She did a Henrietta hyper-sneeze that blew her right over the bed and onto the floor.

"Wow," she shouted. "Look. It must have been blown out by the hyper-sneeze." She pointed. Hanging from the light shade on a piece of string was Henrietta's wobbly tooth.

*   *   *

The next morning Henrietta came downstairs looking very sad.

"What's wrong?" asked Mum. "Didn't the tooth fairy come and take your tooth

away last night?"

Henrietta nodded.

"But she forgot to leave my twenty pence."

Dad looked up from his breakfast.

"Oh yes. I almost forgot. I've got something for you." He reached into his pocket and drew out a small envelope. It was addressed to Henrietta.

Henrietta opened the envelope and took out a piece of paper. She read it aloud.

'Dear Henrietta,

I'm sorry I didn't leave your twenty pence. But your room was so messy that I didn't know where to put it!

Here is a special present for you instead.

From

Mrs. Tooth Fairy'

"But where's my special present?"
cried Henrietta. She turned the envelope
upside down and shook it until, at last,
something fell out and landed on the
table.

"Wow! Fantastic!"

It was her special present. A pair of the
stripiest greenest laces in the whole wide
world.

A SELECTED LIST OF TITLES AVAILABLE FROM YOUNG CORGI

THE PRICES SHOWN BELOW WERE CORRECT AT THE TIME OF GOING TO PRESS. HOWEVER TRANSWORLD PUBLISHERS RESERVE THE RIGHT TO SHOW NEW RETAIL PRICES ON COVERS WHICH MAY DIFFER FROM THOSE PREVIOUSLY ADVERTISED IN THE TEXT OR ELSEWHERE.

☐	52713 0	**ROYAL BLUNDER**	*Henrietta Branford*	£2.50
☐	52524 3	**GREEDY ALICE**	*Helen Cresswell*	£2.50
☐	52301 1	**T.R. BEAR: ENTER T.R.**	*Terrance Dicks*	£2.50
☐	52700 9	**T.R. BEAR: T.R. AT THE ZOO**	*Terrance Dicks*	£2.50
☐	52648 7	**SELENE GOES HOME**	*Lucy Diggs*	£2.50
☐	52614 2	**THE THREE BEARS LEND A HAND**	*Eric Johns*	£2.50
☐	52701 7	**ROLAND AND THE GREEN KNIGHT**	*Ann Jungman*	£2.50
☐	52447 6	**URSULA CAMPING**	*Sheila Lavelle*	£1.75
☐	52664 9	**CALCULATOR ANNIE**	*Alexander McCall Smith*	£2.50
☐	52558 8	**THE SCARY MOUSE**	*Marjorie Newman*	£2.50
☐	52545 6	**PURR**	*Jennifer Zabel*	£2.50

All Young Corgi Books are available at your bookshop or newsagent, or can be ordered from the following address:
Transworld Publishers Ltd,
Cash Sales Department,
P.O. Box 11, Falmouth, Cornwall TR10 9EN

Please send a cheque or postal order (no currency) and allow £1.00 for postage and packing for one book, an additional 50p for a second book, and an additional 30p for each subsequent book ordered to a maximum charge of £3.00 if ordering seven or more books.

Overseas customers, including Eire, please allow £2.00 for postage and packing for the first book, an additional £1.00 for a second book, and an additional 50p for each subsequent title ordered.

NAME (Block Letters) ....

ADDRESS ....

....

SELENE GOES HOME

by Lucy Diggs

'TAKE ME HOME! PLEASE?'

Selene loves the house where she lives. It's a wonderful place for a little cat. But one terrible day her owner, Margaret, moves home – to a *houseboat*. A horrible place! All Selene can see is water and boats and birds. If only she could go home again . . .

Luckily, she meets a cheeky seagull who offers to help. But what will Selene find if she gets back to her old house? Will it still feel like home?

An enchanting tale in which a brave little cat discovers the real meaning of *home*.

SBN 0 552 52648 7

THE THREE BEARS LEND A HAND

by Eric Johns

'Once upon a dark and scary night three fearless bears crept out of their bedrooms . . .'

Barleycorn, Honeycomb, and Bumble Bear live in a house with three children, one little girl for each bear to look after. When the children are unhappy (they have run out of sweets), the three brave bears make a plan to help – and set off on an exciting adventure.

Read about what happened – in the bears' own words – as Barleycorn, Honeycomb and Bumble write down the story of their great adventure.

SBN 0 552 52614 2

YOUNG CORGI

T.R. BEAR: ENTER T.R.
by Terrance Dicks

It all started when Jimmy got a parcel from his Uncle Colin in America. The teddy bear inside was unlike any bear Jimmy had ever seen. He looked tough, and he was wearing glasses! According to the label, his name was Theodore Roosevelt – T.R. for short.

Jimmy soon finds out that life with T.R. Bear is quite eventful . . .

SBN 0 552 52301 1

YOUNG CORGI